A HAT So Simple

For Leslie Bauman and Bonnie Brook.
— J.S.

Copyright © 1993 by Jerry Smath.

Published by Troll Associates, Inc.
First published in hardcover by Bridgewater Books.

Designed by Leslie Bauman.

10 9 8 7 6 5 4 3 2

Library of Congress Cataloging-in-Publication Data

Smath, Jerry.
A hat so simple / by Jerry Smath.
p. cm.
Summary: Edna the alligator has quite an adventure when she
goes to buy a hat to wear while fishing with her husband Paul.
ISBN 0-8167-3016-4. — ISBN 0-8167-3017-2 (pbk.)
[1. Alligators—Fiction. 2. Hats—Fiction. 3. Stories in rhyme.]
I. Title.
PZ8.3.S64Hat 1993 93-22205
[E]—dc20

A HAT So Simple

BY JERRY SMATH

Troll Medallion

Paul said to Edna, "Fish with me!
You'll find it very pleasant."
He gave his wife a fishing pole
And said, "This is your present."

Edna thanked her husband
For the fishing pole he bought her.
"Let's go fishing now!" she said.
So they ran down to the water.

While they sat there fishing
The time just seemed to fly,
And soon the day got hotter
As the sun rose in the sky.

Edna turned to Paul and said,
"The sun's too hot today!
I need a hat upon my head
Or soon I'll faint away!"

Paul gave his hat to Edna
But she didn't like its looks.
His hat was old and smelly
And had too many hooks.

"I'll buy my own!" said Edna.
"One that's small and neat.
So when I'm fishing in the sun
I will not feel the heat."

Edna went to buy a hat
While Paul fished from the shore.
She crossed the bridge to town and found
The store of Miss LaBoar.

"I WANT THAT HAT!" said Edna.
"The one that's small and neat.
So when I'm fishing in the sun
I will not feel the heat."

Miss LaBoar, who owned the store, said,
"No! That hat won't do!
But try this big one on for size.
I feel it's really you."

She put a hat on Edna's head
That nearly touched the floor.
And Edna, without thinking,
Just paid and left the store.

Now, Edna wasn't certain
About the hat she'd bought.
So when she met two friends of hers,
She asked them what they thought.

Her friends, the Duckworth sisters,
Both liked to give advice.
They liked to give advice so much,
They sometimes gave it twice.

The Duckworth sisters both agreed.
Their comments were the same.
"Your hat's not really big at all,
It simply is too plain."

Holly reached into her bag
And from a stack of books,
Took a satin bow and said,
"Try this one on for looks."

"Still too plain!" said Dolly.
"But look what I have got—
A great big yellow daisy!
Please excuse the pot."

"How nice of you," said Edna,
"To make my hat so grand.
Maybe I was wrong to want
A hat that was so bland."

Then the sisters said, "Good-bye."
And after they departed,
Edna noticed that her hat
Weighed more than when she started.

Edna turned and started home,
Walking with great care,
When, in the woods, she saw two friends,
Big Bert and Sarah Bear.

Both bears were busy eating
A great big picnic lunch.
Sipping soup and munching grapes,
Often by the bunch.

Edna pointed to the hat
That flopped atop her head.
She asked the big bear what he thought
And this is what he said . . .

"Your hat could use some purple grapes!
Just trust your old friend Bert.
Not only are they pretty
But they make a fine dessert."

"You could be right," said Edna.
"It is a long trip back.
Maybe I'll be hungry
And want a little snack."

"Take my balloon. It's pretty too!"
Said little Sarah Bear.
"Won't you put it on your hat?
I've filled it up with air."

Edna thanked the friendly bears
And wobbled down the road.
The simple hat she went to buy
Was now a heavy load.

But Edna kept on going,
Till she met a man called Brite,
Who said, "Please buy a candle.
You'll find my price is right."

"I don't need a candle, sir,"
Said Edna with a sigh.
"Oh, yes you do!" said Mister Brite.
"And I will tell you why...

"Your hat is fine in daytime,
As long as there is light.
But you will need this candle
To light your way at night."

"If it's needed," Edna said,
"Then I won't disagree.
For now I'm not so certain
What the best thing is for me."

So, with the candle on her hat,
And trying not to fall,
Edna walked the best she could
And hurried home to Paul.

Now the sky was getting dark.
Her hat grew hard to handle.
So Edna said, "Before I fall
I'll stop and light my candle."

Then, in the sky, some birds flew by,
And thought it would be neat,
If they all sat on Edna's hat,
And had some grapes to eat.

"No! No!" she shouted bravely.
"Drat you birds! Shoo! Scat!
This is not your dinner.
This is my new hat!"

The way the birds ate Edna's grapes
Was really quite appalling.
They made her trip and lose her grip
And then she started falling.

Edna landed with a splash,
With no one there to save her.
She almost drowned, but then she found
The gift that Sarah gave her.

The balloon kept Edna floating
With her flower, pot and all.
But the current pulled her faster
Toward an awful waterfall.

"Double drat!" cried Edna,
When she heard the water roar.
"If this hat were smaller,
I could swim to shore!"

The waterfall was closer now,
So Edna gave a scream.
Her frantic call was heard by Paul,
Still fishing in the stream.

"I hear you Edna!" shouted Paul.
"And I can see your light.
I'll cast my fishing line to you—
Just grab, and hold on tight!"

Paul pulled on his fishing pole,
And then he pulled some more,
Until he saw that Edna
Was safely on the shore.

When Paul saw Edna standing there
He asked, "What have you done?
That hat is much too big for you.
Why, it must weigh a ton!

"You went to buy a simple hat,
At least that's what I thought.
But if that's so, then tell me why
That hat is what you bought."

Edna knew that Paul was right.
When morning came she quickly hiked
Back to the store of Miss LaBoar
To buy the hat she *really* liked.

Now Paul *and* Edna like to fish.
They do so *every* day.
And, if by chance you meet them,
You may hear Edna say...

"I love my hat so simple.
It is so small and neat.
Now when I'm fishing in the sun,
I never feel the heat."